MR. FLOPSY

WHISPERS FROM GOD

A LESSON ON BEING STILL

Christi Eley

For information regarding permissions, contact the publisher at:

Cottontail Publishing
5748 Remington Drive
Winston-Salem, NC 217104

www.mrscottontailandfriends.com

Author: Christi Eley   Illustrator: Aries Cheung

ISBN Paperback: 978-1-7359680-3-2
ISBN Hardcover: 978-1-7359680-0-1

First Edition 2021
Published in the United States of America
Printed in the United States of America

This book is dedicated to my loving family,
Mark, Erin, Sydney, and all the people and
animals who inspired me along the way.

A special thank you to E.P.

Cam loves to run around. Every day, Cam is racing here and there looking for fun things to do – moving, playing, running.

Sometimes Cam makes a lot of noise as he goes. Everything sounds so good to him – talking, yelling, asking questions.

But every day, Cam's parents, grandparents and teachers say the same thing – slow down, sit still and be quiet!

Cam doesn't understand why they say this. Don't they like having fun? Why does he have to STOP!

BE STILL
AND KNOW THAT
I AM GOD...

PSALM 46:10

Cam hears people say this. Cam wishes he knew what it meant.

Maybe Cam's best friend, Mr. Flopsy, will know. Cam thinks Mr. Flopsy is very smart!

BE STILL
AND KNOW THAT
I AM GOD...

Cam looks over at Mr. Flopsy. He is sitting so quietly and being so still.

How does he do this? Cam knows that Mr. Flopsy loves to hop around.

Mr. Flopsy is in his favorite comfy spot. He loves to breathe in and out very slowly, and his whiskers barely move.

Cam asks Mr. Flopsy, "How do you sit so still and quiet when there is so much noise – the dog barking, people talking loudly, and me running all around."

NOISE! NOISE! NOISE!

Mr. Flopsy whispers, "I stay still and quiet while I think of my favorite things.

"I love my veggie garden with all my favorite foods. I especially enjoy the orange carrots with the green leafy tops.

"And I love my flower garden with all the beautiful smells and colors. The yellow roses and pink pansies are just extraordinary.

"What are some of your favorite things, Cam?"

Cam moves closer to Mr. Flopsy, "What happens when you are bored and want to hop around and play, but you are stuck in your cage and have to wait."

PATIENCE! PATIENCE! PATIENCE!

PATIENCE!

PATIENCE!

PATIENCE!

Mr. Flopsy replies, "I have learned to wait and be patient. I know that I will get to hop around soon and do my binkies (big happy jumps), so I dream of the time I will be doing these fun things.

"Just the thought of getting to do a binkie makes me smile all over."

Cam moves very close to Mr. Flopsy and nervously asks, "Do you ever feel scared when you are all alone and don't know what is going to happen?"

SCARED! SCARED! SCARED!

Mr. Flopsy calmly replies, "That sometimes is very hard. But the thing that helps me the most is thinking of you holding me. I feel so safe and love that the most.

"Wrapped in my special blanket, held close to your heart, I feel like you are giving me a long endless hug that will keep me safe forever."

Cam raises his voice and asks Mr. Flopsy, "Do you ever worry about things? I worry all the time about what is going to happen later today, tomorrow or some day!"

WORRY! WORRY! WORRY!

Mr. Flopsy lovingly looks at Cam and says, "I trust that you will always take care of me. And I can hear your sweet words in my head. They are so comforting, and then I don't worry.

"I delight in hearing you say, 'I love you,' 'You are such a good rabbit,' 'I will be with you always.'"

Cam starts feeling good all over. Everything feels clearer, brighter and more peaceful now.

Cam lovingly looks over at Mr. Flopsy and watches him slowly breath in and out. He can just barely see his whiskers moving.

QUIET, QUIET, QUIET.

Mr. Flopsy feels good all over. His thoughts are slowly drifting away. He is ready to do "The Flop," which means he is happy beyond words.

There is nothing else he needs to do at this moment, but just BE.

HAPPY! HAPPY! HAPPY!

Cam is happy sitting in this comfy place now. Slowly breathing in and out. Maybe he understands what it means to be still now.

He imagines blowing his thoughts away in the wind. You don't always have to be doing something.

When you slow down, be still and quiet....

You learn to listen, trust and feel loved by God.

BE STILL
AND KNOW THAT I
AM GOD...

PSALM 46:10

Cam likes this.

Mr. Flopsy is so smart!

BUT ASK
THE ANIMALS,
AND THEY WILL
TEACH YOU...

JOB 12:7

Additional Suggestions to Help Children be Still and Quiet:

- Repeat *Psalm 46:10* whenever child is feeling anxious or upset. This will be a repetitive prayer that will help ease their mind and realize that they are not alone

- Find their own comfy spot with pillows and blankets and favorite things

- Close their eyes and think of something that makes them happy

- Listen to soothing music

- Hold something special in their hand

- Count to 10 and then backwards from 10

- Think of the five senses – something they love to see, smell, hear, taste and touch

- Say their favorite prayer and repeat several times

- Sit and spend time with their pet (if they have one)

Additional Bible Verses for Each Lesson in the Book:

- **For the Lesson of Quiet -**

  "My soul, wait in silence for God only, for my hope is from him."
  Psalm 62:5

- **For the Lesson of Patience -**

  "I waited patiently for the Lord, he turned to me and heard my cry."
  Psalm 40:1

- **For the Lesson of Being Scared –**

  "This is my command, be strong and courageous! Do not be afraid or discouraged. For the Lord your God is with you wherever you go."
  Joshua 1:9

- **For the Lesson of Worry –**

  "Don't worry about anything; instead, pray about everything. Tell God what you need and thank him for all that he has done."
  Phillipians 4:6-7

- **For the Lesson of Being Happy –**

  "Rejoice in the Lord always; again I will say, rejoice!"

  Philippians 4:4

BE STILL
AND KNOW THAT
I AM GOD...

PSALM 46:10

If you were inspired by this book, we would love for you to leave a review on the site where you purchased the book!

We would love for you to invite your friends to check out **Mrs. Cottontail and Friends**.

Thank you so much for spreading Mr. Flopsy's warm fuzzy message to children everywhere!

Please visit our website at
www.mrscottontailandfriends.com
for upcoming announcements!

And check out our Facebook page at
https://www.facebook.com/mrscottontailandfriends

Also look for the following Mr. Flopsy
activities on our website:

- Free Mr. Flopsy Coloring Pages
- Mrs. Cottontail and Friends Workbook
- Mrs. Cottontail and Friends Virtual Parties and Story Times with Videos and Zoom
- Mrs. Cottontail and Friends Streaming of Bunny Time

Children will love to see Mr. Flosy and his friends up close via these virtual opportunities!

CPSIA information can be obtained
at www.ICGtesting.com
Printed in the USA
LVHW070318190121
676859LV00016B/408

9 781735 968001